Farm
of Fear

Ladybird

Published by Ladybird Books Ltd 2012
A Penguin Company
Penguin Books Ltd, 80 Strand, London, WC2R 0RL, UK
Penguin Books Australia Ltd, Camberwell, Victoria, Australia
Penguin Group (NZ), 67 Apollo Drive, Rosedale, Auckland
0632, New Zealand (a division of Pearson New Zealand Ltd)

"Who Needs a Hug?", "Nothing in the Dark",
"The Surprise" and "Farm of Fear"
written by Greg Farshtey

AMEET Produced by AMEET Sp. z o.o.
under license from the LEGO Group.

AMEET Sp. z o.o.,
Przybyszewskiego 176/178, 93-120 Łódź – Poland
ameet@ameet.com.pl
www.ameet.pl

Penguin Books Ltd, 80 Strand, London, WC2R 0RL, UK
Please keep the Penguin Books Ltd address for future reference.
www.LEGO.com

ISBN: 9781409313991
001 - 10 9 8 7 6 5 4 3 2 1
Printed in Poland

Item name: LEGO® Ninjago. Farm of Fear / Nothing in the Dark
Series: LNR
Item number: LNR 8/LNR 7
Batch: 01/GB

Contents

The Union of Snakes

After betraying my nephew, Lloyd Garmadon, Pythor continued to wreak havoc on Ninjago. While I took Lloyd into my care, Pythor opened another snake tomb and released one more snake tribe, the Venomari. With his cunning persuasion and stolen Sacred Flute (an ancient weapon designed to combat the powers of snakes), Pythor united the four tribes under his rule. The last of the Anacondrai was one step closer to destroying Ninjago.

Fatal Illusion

The Venomari are neither the strongest nor the wisest of the snake tribes. However, they have an incredibly dangerous ability: they can spit toxic venom that makes their victims hallucinate. These victims see things that do not exist and hear words that have not been said. Their darkest fears cloud their minds, causing them to become disorientated and helpless. It doesn't last forever, but it creates a perfect opportunity for a snake to strike. Keep a safe distance when you meet the Venomari and, if they start to spit – get out of the way!

The Surprise

Spitta and Lizaru were hiding in the bushes along the side of a forest road. As an experienced Venomari warrior, Lizaru had been on many ambushes like this one. True, waiting for ninja was a little trickier than pouncing on unsuspecting villagers, but the game was still the same: spring, spit, battle over.

His partner, Spitta, was much more anxious than he was.

"What if they don't come?" asked Spitta.

"They'll come," Lizaru whispered. "Keep your voice down."

Spitta said something back, but no sound came out of his mouth. Lizaru glared at him. "Not that low, now I can't hear you!"

"I said," Spitta repeated, "what if they spot us?"

"That's why we're behind bushes," Lizaru explained. "If they look this way, they'll see shrubbery...not snakes. We're going to give them a big surprise!"

Spitta smiled, his forked tongue darting out of his mouth. "Right. So we spit our venom at them, they go all crazy, and we win."

"That's how it works, yes."

Spitta's smile faded. "Hmmmm. What if my mouth goes dry just as the fight starts?"

"Sshhhh!" Lizaru said. "They're coming!"

Spitta peered through the branches. Two ninja were coming down the road, one dressed in red and one dressed in black. They were younger than he had expected. Both were carrying golden weapons, one a sword and the other a scythe. Spitta suddenly wished there were more Venomari around.

"These are the guys who whirl stuff around, aren't they?" Spitta whispered.

"Spinjitzu, yeah," answered Lizaru, never taking his eyes from his prey. "Just wait until they stop spinning. Maybe they'll be dizzy."

The ninja came closer. They seemed to have no idea what was waiting for them. "Not yet," said Lizaru. "Not yet ... not yet ... now!"

Lizaru leapt out of the bushes, with Spitta following awkwardly behind. Lizaru reared back and spat his hallucinogenic venom at the black-garbed ninja. But the ninja had already taken a step back and he dodged the attack with ease. The ninja in red, Kai, was swinging a flaming sword and laughing.

"Only two of you?" said the Ninja of Fire. "That's not even a challenge."

"I knew we needed more snakes!" shouted Spitta, trying and failing to spit at Kai. "Hold still!"

"Personally, I think we have all the snakes we need," said Cole, using his weapon to drive Lizaru back. "We could use a few less."

"How? How did you know we were here?" Lizaru angrily demanded.

Kai faked a kick and landed a double chop on Spitta, knocking the snake on its back. Looking up at the sky, Spitta could see another ninja, this one in blue, gliding through the air with a makeshift pair of wooden wings.

"Um, Lizaru?" he said. "Either they have a really ugly pet bird, or one of the ninja knows how to fly."

Lizaru wasn't listening. He had a plan. Cole's attention was fixed on the snake's head, watching to see when and where he would spit next. Instead, Lizaru lashed out with his right leg, knocking Cole to the ground. Before the ninja could recover, Lizaru had wrestled the golden Scythe of Quakes away from him.

"I have it!" he cried. "I have a weapon of Spinjitzu!"

"Not for long," said Kai. He hurled the Dragon Sword of Fire into the air and charged at Spitta, coming in low and lifting the snake off the ground. He then hurled the Venomari at Lizaru. Just as the two snakes collided, Kai caught the falling sword.

Lizaru was bowled over by his flying partner and fell backwards. The head of the scythe struck the ground. Instantly, a violent earthquake shook the whole area.

"Oh, now you've done it," said Cole. Just like Sensei Wu had

taught him, he rolled across the ground, riding the tremors and letting them carry him toward the two snakes. When he got close, a snapping dragon thrust to Lizaru's upper arm made him drop the scythe. Cole grabbed the weapon before it hit the ground.

"Spitta, get him!" commanded Lizaru.

The other snake charged, but at Kai instead of Cole, thinking the attack might come as a surprise. Caught off-guard, Kai knew his best chance was Spinjitzu. He began to whirl, faster and faster, forming a fiery vortex that swept Spitta off the ground.

"I hate this!" Spitta yelled. "I really hate this!"

When Kai stopped abruptly, Spitta was flung halfway down the road. Lizaru had staggered back up by then, and found himself faced with two armed ninja.

"You planned the ambush, Venomari, but it was you who got the surprise," said Cole. "Run back to your general. Tell him that when the ninja come for him, it won't be a sneak attack. We'll just walk in and take him."

Spitta repeated the message over and over to himself all the way back to the den to make sure he wouldn't forget it. When they got in front of General Acidicus, though, Lizaru just reported that they hadn't seen any ninja all day.

When Spitta asked him why he had lied, Lizaru said, "Who knows what the general would have done if I told him what happened? I don't know about you, Spitta, but I'm sick of surprises."

Incredible Snake Facts

The beauty of learning is that it never stops: you can discover exciting new information at any point.

1. Snakes hibernate during winter. They hide in caves, holes in the ground, cracks in rocks or enclosed bird nests. Sometimes hundreds of hibernating snakes can be found in one place.

2. Some snakes, such as the Asian *vine snake*, have binocular vision, with both eyes capable of focusing on the same point. Their eyes are also unique in the reptile world for their keyhole-shaped pupils.

3. Snakes have different types of teeth, but the African *egg-eating snake* has no teeth at all. It has bony protrusions used for breaking egg shells. They are located on the inside of the snake's spine!

4. Some snakes can smell with their noses but all snakes smell with their forked tongues. Snakes have a small notch in their lips to stick their tongues through, so they don't even need to open their mouths.

5. Most snakes have only one functioning lung, and the other is usually greatly reduced because there isn't enough room for it in the snake's elongated body.

6. Fangs are usually in the front part of a snake's upper jaw. Snakes with really long fangs have a smart self-protection mechanism – their fangs fold back into the mouth so they don't bite themselves!

Sensei Wu asks

Snakes never stop surprising me. Some snakes can actually fly! True or false?

Answer: True. Some snakes are capable of flying. The Asian paradise flying snake launches itself from a tree, sucks in its belly and spreads its ribs to make its body as flat as possible. Gliding through the air, the body of the snake flexes alternately to the left and right to stabilize the flight. The snake can fly like this for up to a hundred metres, depending on the height it jumps from.

Snake Jokes

Jay loves to joke about everything. Even though we have four snake tribes as enemies now, he always has a good joke to cheer the team up.

What do you get if you cross two snakes with a magic spell ? Addercadabra and abradacobra!

"Hissss is the most absent-minded snake I've ever known," says one snake to another. "Why?" "He keeps losing his skin."

What do you do if you find a snake in your bed? Sleep in the bathtub!

What do you get if you cross a snake and a hot dog? A fangfurter.

What subject do snakes enjoy at school? Hissss-tory.

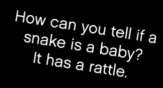

How can you tell if a snake is a baby? It has a rattle.

What do you do if you find a python in your toilet? Wait until he's finished!

How do snakes show they love you? They give you hugs and hisses!

One snake asks another: "Remind me, are we the venomous type?" "Why do you ask?" "I just bit my lip!"

Sensei Wu asks

A venomous snake does not have to worry if it bites itself, as its own venom will not cause it any harm. True or false?

Answer: True. Snakes generally tend to be immune to the venom of their own species, but their resistance to other species' venoms varies greatly.

Farm of Fear

Kai, Zane and Jay trudged down a muddy road just after dawn. The air was already hot and humid. The only sounds were the ninja's feet hitting the wet ground and the calls of birds. Jay couldn't help but think about his straw mat and warm blanket back at camp.

"I know we had to make this trip," he said. "But did we have to do it this early?"

"Sensei Wu says the Venomari are in the area," Zane replied. "They can do great damage with their venom. It makes you hallucinate! We can't afford to let them roam free."

"Easy for you to say," Jay grumbled. "You're always up before sunrise anyway."

"Argue later," Kai interrupted. "I see the village up ahead."

The town wasn't very big. It was just a collection of houses and barns surrounded by a lot of farmland. All three ninja knew places like this well. The villagers might not have a lot of luxuries or live in big homes, but they would love their town as much as any city dweller. Hopefully, they would welcome the help of the ninja to rid their area of Venomari.

"I bet they offer us a nice breakfast," said Jay, forgetting how tired he was by focusing on his hunger. "I bet Cole wishes he were here."

"I am sure they will give us what they can spare, but that may not be very much," Zane replied. "It is not yet harvest time. As for Cole, that Constrictai attack will keep him out of action for a few more days, at least."

"We'll tell him all about it when we get back," said Kai. "Let's go, and watch out for snakes."

The three friends were almost at the border of the town when they heard rustling in the fields on either side. The ninja, expecting a snake attack, drew their weapons and curled their hands into fists.

"Finally!" said one villager. "We've been looking all over for you!"

"You have?" asked Kai. Not even the ninja had known they were coming to this village until that morning.

A second farmer gestured toward the ninja with his pitchfork. "Don't waste time talking to them, Sam. Just get them back to the village."

"I know, Jin," said Sam. "The wife wants to have them for dinner tomorrow night, remember?"

Jay smiled at Zane. Dinner sounded pretty good to him.

"We're ninja working for Sensei Wu," Zane explained to the farmers. "We are here to rid the area of Venomari. Have you seen any?"

Zane was amazed when the farmers completely ignored his questions. Instead of answering, they began prodding the ninja with their pitchforks, herding them toward the village.

"Hey!" Jay snapped, when he was almost poked by one of the tools. "Watch where you're sticking that thing!"

"What's going on here?" Kai demanded. "We're here to help you!"

"They sure do make a lot of noise, don't they?" laughed Jin. "Almost like they know what's going to happen to them."

Now the ninja could see where they were being led: a large, empty pigsty near a barn. The floor of the pen was muddy and covered in footprints.

"Whatever they do, just go along with it for now," Zane said quietly. "They have been infected by the Venomari. I can see it in their eyes."

"You mean they're hallucinating?" asked Jay.

"Yes," said Zane. "I gather they are seeing us as escaped farm animals. Most interesting."

"So when they say they want to have us for dinner..." Kai began.

"Indeed," said Zane. "They really do want to have us for dinner."

The three ninja allowed themselves to be prodded into the pen, and watched as the farmers closed the gate behind them. The fence was low enough that they could easily climb over it, if they had to. All they would have to do was wait for the farmers to leave.

"You stay here," Jin said to Sam. "Make sure they don't run off again."

"Oh, great," muttered Kai. "Zane, how long does the effect of Venomari venom last?"

"That depends on a number of factors: amount of venom, length of exposure, purity of the venom concentration, wind speed and direction –"

"What he means is, he doesn't know," said Jay. "Well, I don't intend to stand around waiting for supper time. Let's get out of here."

Jay started toward the fence, followed by Kai and Zane. The farmer raised his pitchfork. Jay was already

calculating how he could get the farmer out of the way without hurting him. He was just about to make his move when he heard Zane saying, "We have another problem!"

The three ninja turned to see mud on the ground of the pigpen moving on its own. Suddenly, three Venomari erupted from beneath the surface, hissing angrily at Jay and the others.

"Oh, boy," said Jay. "I think we know now why the pigs ran away."

"The Venomari needed to cool off in the heat of the day," said Zane, pulling out one of his shurikens. "So they took refuge under the mud of the pen."

Zane tossed his shuriken at the ground, turning the mud to ice. The snakes found themselves trapped, but were still able to spit venom at their foes. Kai scooped up loose fragments of ice and formed them into a ball, then threw it at the nearest snake. It hit the Venomari right in the mouth, knocking him backward.

"Let's see you spit with your mouth full," Kai said, sliding across the ice and into battle.

The ninja heard a yelp from behind them. The farmer had awakened from his trance, only to see three ninja battling three man-sized snakes in his pigsty. He ran for help.

Jay narrowly dodged a spray of venom, which hit the shoulder of his robe. "Oh, come on!" he yelled. "I just had this cleaned."

"You will soon be outnumbered," Zane said to the three snakes. "When the villagers return, you will be captured or destroyed. Better to surrender now."

The snakes began to make a strange, shrill noise, and then tore themselves free from the ice. Kai realized with a sick feeling in his stomach that the Venomari were laughing.

He soon found out why. About a dozen more snakes were converging on the pen from all directions. The ninja were surrounded. The Venomari began to rock back and forth, getting ready to spit their venom on Kai, Zane and Jay.

"Well, I guess we can say we found the snakes," said Jay.

"Yeah, we're getting a little too good at that," Kai replied.

"It would be best if we avoided the Venomari attack," Zane put in. "There is no telling what that much venom might do."

"Right," said Kai, with a smile. "No telling. Why don't we ask the Venomari?"

Now Jay was smiling. "A little taste of their own medicine? I like it."

The Venomari reared back to spit. Just as they started forward, the three ninja whirled into Spinjitzu tornadoes. Before the snakes could react, the fierce power of the whirlwinds had blown the venom right back at its source. The ninja surged

forward, their vortex
shattering the gate to
firewood as they
escaped from the pen.

When they were a few
hundred yards away, the
ninja stopped to prepare
for the fight. Behind them,
villagers armed with clubs,
rocks, and farm tools were
rushing up to help. They eyed
the snakes warily, waiting for
the Venomari to attack.

Finally, one of the snakes
turned and slithered a few feet toward the ninja and
the villagers. It glanced from one to the other, then
said, "Moo."

"Moo?" Jay repeated.

"I don't believe it," said Kai.

"Oink," said another of the Venomari. "Oink oink."

Three of the other snakes were now pecking at the
ground and making clucking noises. A small group of
others were saying "baa" and looking for fresh grass to
eat. One had actually broken into the closest thing a
snake could do to a gallop. In fact, none of the snakes
were acting anything like snakes.

"Incredible," said Zane. "Exposure to their own venom, plus the surrounding environment, has convinced these Venomari they are farm animals. They believe they are cows, horses, sheep, pigs...even chickens."

"Well, that's good," said Sam, smiling. "We could use the eggs."

* * *

The villagers treated the ninja to a wonderful dinner. When their stomachs were full, the heroes started the long journey back to camp.

"That was quite an adventure," said Kai. "I've never been mistaken for a pig before."

Jay chuckled. "Oh, I could say something here...but I won't."

"The Venomari are more dangerous than we believed," said Zane. "Let us hope the chains we bound them with will hold until the Sensei tells us what we should do with them."

"Well, I know one thing," said Jay.

"What's that?" said Kai.

"At breakfast tomorrow...I think I might skip the bacon."

Even Zane almost smiled at that.

Fighting Back

Since Pythor stole the sacred flute from my ninja, Jay has never ceased to surprise us with his truly ingenious anti-snake inventions. His efforts have been admirable, but haven't always gone to plan...

Sonic Snake Repellent

This device produced a sound that discouraged snakes from coming to villages. Inaudible to other creatures, the sound somehow attracted lava–spitting ash bats that came looking for its source and accidentally burned crops...and the invention itself.

Snake Sleeping Dust

This mix of secret ninja dusts had no effect on snakes, but made some plants mutate into a nasty combination of sleepy willows and groovy vines. The mutant plants grabbed farmers and lulled them into a deep sleep. On the bright side, the dust got rid of all the weeds.

Scaresnake

Jay built a few mock-up dragons and placed them in farmers' fields to scare snakes away. It turned out, though, that snakes actually liked them and stole them all. Now they keep the scaresnakes in their lairs like precious pieces of art.

Portable Hissodetector

This device warned of approaching snakes by detecting their hiss. Unfortunately, it could not tell the difference between the hiss of snakes and the sound of lisping farmer children. Several false alarms later, Jay got rid of it.

Sensei Wu asks

Sadly, Jay's inventions always turn out to be failures, just like the dragon roar amplifier or the Nunchucks of Lightning he had built earlier. True or false?

Answer: False. Firstly, Jay did not invent the Nunchucks of Lightning. Secondly, it wasn't a failure, and neither was the dragon roar amplifier. It worked fine. Just ask the Lightning Dragon!

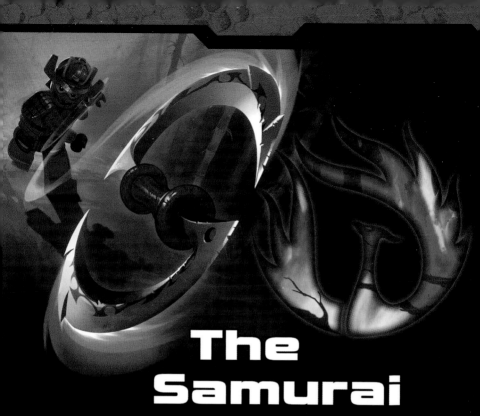

The Samurai

As if from nowhere, Ninjago suddenly had a new hero!
A mysterious Samurai appeared to fight the Serpentine.
He was strong, super-swift and even more skilled than
my ninja. But was this masked warrior friend or foe?
One thing was clear: the Samurai hated the Serpentine.
My ninja began to complain about this competing hero
and, despite their greatest efforts, remained unaware of
his true identity. But I knew that iron would sharpen iron,
and that the competition would serve them well.

Ninja Quiz

Let's see if the Venomari venom has distorted your memory ... or sense of reality ...

1. Which two Venomari prepared an ambush for the ninja?

2. What was Spitta worried about before the ninja arrived?

3. How many ninja actually took part in the battle?

4. Who wrestled the Scythe of Quakes away from Cole?

5. What did Lizaru report to the Venomari general?

6. Who didn't take part in the mission on the farm?

7. What kind of animal did the villagers think the ninja were?

8. Why did the ninja not fight the hallucinating villagers?

9. Where did the ninja fight the Venomari?

10. How did the ninja defeat the snakes on the farm?